AF284356

Sunday 9. Oktober 2022.

Hey friends,

Please forgive me for having spelling and grammatical mistakes in my texts. At least in the German books, laugh. I grew up speaking and writing English since my childhood. German spelling and grammar was never my forte. I never wrote any books before 2021/2022 either. Thank you and happy reading.

Your, B. E. Wasner.

B. E. Wasner

Can Dreams Come True - Or Do You Believe In Love At First Sight?

A Book with Two Stories!

Witten & Translated from the German Original Story by B. E. Wasner.

Title of the Original Story "Können Träume Wahr Werden?" B. E. Wasner

A FANTASY NOVEL

Imprint

Bibliographic information from the German National Library: The German National Library lists this publication in the German National Bibliography; detailed bibliographic data can be accessed on the Internet at http://dnb.dnb.de.

© 2022 B. E. Wasner

Produced and published by: BoD – Books on Demand, Norderstedt

ISBN: 978-3-7557-7762-5

Special thanks to my wonderful girlfriend in the United States for proofreading this book for me. I love you Sis. ♥ ☺ ☼

And thanks to my wonderful bookstore ladies, for telling me where to go to with my stories to get them printed.

Table of Contents:

Novel #1.

Brief description:

It's about friendship, trust, love & the relationship between two different women, and the con-
flicts of everyday life even with sexuality in the
background, encounters with everyday problems, contact with disabled people & the asso-
ciated willingness to help.

Novel Nr. 1:

My Adventures on the MS Lucky Charm.

Chapter 1

My adventures on the MS Lucky Charm started with good luck! I won a Mediterranean cruise in a competition. It is for 4-weeks! Despite of my handicap. I have been told by the shipping company that I can get support for the things I need help with if they know soon enough. Everything went well, my doctor allowed me to go. I had my medications and medication plan, foreign health certificate & health insurance card, vaccination card & vaccinations, also tetanus booster, health certificate, passport etc. Mobile phone plus charging cable, laptop with accessories, power wheelchair and charger and whatever else that was on the list. The day of arrival was a chaos day. Arriving and check in was ok and then it happened; my power wheelchair was gone! Simply gone, untraceable! As if swallowed up by the ground. Then a cook had to be hospitalized with an acute appendix, the second cook also had an accident, when he left his house he fell and broke his arm. As we needed quickly a replacement we were offered a short shore leave but were brought back on the ship so quickly that they almost forgot me. They said the ship was delayed but everyone needed to get back on board just the same. That was when Head stewardess Marion suddenly noticed that I was not in the group because I could not keep up so fast. Not only had our hand luggage been taken away from us, but also my power wheelchair, so unfortunately I did not come along with them. Even though I am disabled and need my wheelchair, but it was gone! Stewardess Marion then waited for me and took me back to the ship. Then she remembered that the shipping company had said that there was a disabled woman on board and that she needs help with a few things from time to time. In addition, that she has her power wheelchair with her because she depends on it, especially on long trips so that nobody has to push her normal wheelchair. Marion was not aware at this time that it could be me as I could still walk, only slowly. Stewardess Tanja, Marion's right hand, had conjured up a spontaneous kiosk sale as compensation for the late departure and was in the process of setting it up, as we got back on board. Suddenly I was not feeling so well and I said that I have to go to the toilet please. Marion took me there and I asked her if she could please wait? I do not want to get lost, I was afraid of losing my way. She said yes of course and she took my Walkman and other things for a moment. Yes I still have something like that, laugh. Then suddenly Itold her that it is not easy for me to ask for help with some things, like with showering or bathing, especially because I am not like most women in a way. Marion knew immediately what I meant and felt honored that I had enough trust in her to say that from the beginning of the trip. I do not know why I did that either. My inner voice just told me to tell her, it might be right for later help.

We were told that all luggages have to stay on board, including handbags and backpacks, even my power wheelchair, everything. Even if that was stupid with the power wheelchair.

When we entered the big hall, Tanja came towards us with small plastic bags. That is when Marion called her over because she saw this and I almost lost my Walkman and the other stuff I was holding.

Tanja came over to us. She had already prepared half of the table with biscuits and other sweets, fruits and pretzel sticks for (normal healthy) people. Diabetics should get the same things that where made for them set up on the other part of the table and both should get water to drink. The areas were separated by some space and tablecloths. Because it was very hot, there were no chocolates, or dairy products, but soft drinks for everyone. Mineral water, ice tea, soda and coca cola with and without sugar in the small machine PET-bottles, as well as juices. BUT! Nothing with alcohol! AND! No energy drinks! I was asked what I wanted. Then after my name was checked off on a copy of the passengierlist, Marion asked Tanja to take me to my seat. As the people sitting in the first row saw that I could not walk very good, they changed seats so I could sit in the front. This way they were also near there friends. Only this list did not say that I am disabled, or that I am the winner of the Cruise contest. Tanja wanted to give me my kiosk bag, but I said no, that is not fair, when I get my bag just because I was standing up here with both of you, before the other people do not even know what is going on. With this list the people were asked are you diabetic "yes" or "no"? So that they know to which stewardess they have to go to. My name was written onto the bag and put into a box until later. Then as Tanja took me to my seat, Marion told those waiting what she and Tanja were going to do and it would start in a few minutes. Everyone but the children were now in the big hall, the children had their own program with childcare. As I went to my seat with Tanja, I asked very quietly how that could work, just two stewardesses, standing at two tables, asking all the people what they wanted, packing the bags, looking for the drinks and collecting the cash too? All at the same time? The things were not free. You two are not squids! There should be at least 2 more people there, 1 person who is with Marion and 1 person who is with you. It would be even better if there were 4 more people here, 2 more for the drinks too. And if one more suggestion is allowed, I would divide the two tables with the drinks drawing the line. There are these cardboard pallets or whatever where these Coca Cola cans, 7 Up, Dr. Pepper, etc. sit on when they are in the store or when you buy the whole batch at once. One I believe is red and the other green. If you put 2-4 of them up on the table, you not only have the separation for the first, but also space for many cans at hand. The water is the same for everyone. Suddenly Tanja was very pale and when she saw that 3 helpers were standing next to Marion, she said loud that they should please stay there. As they waited, they said what about our group leader? Let that be my concern said Marion. Then you can tell him that right away, he is coming and Markus is with him. Not only that Marion & Tanja thought, because they had seen something else too. Markus had 4 cardboard pallets in his hands. Tanja had just told Marion about my concerns.

The temporary assistant cook wanted to know where the helpers were staying.

Because the 3 young people and Markus where in contrast to him, a part of the MS Lucky Charm crew and are training as jumpers to see where they fit in best. And they know who Head stewardess Marion is, even without her Name-tag that was broken. She had not had the time to get it fixed yet! Marion was just telling him that the 3 of them are staying where they are and so is Markus, plus the cardboard pallets. The temporary assistant cook just said he did not think the helpers would stay as the skipper and head steward joined the little group. The cook did not know them either, just like Marion. The assistant cook was just saying again that he wanted to take the four young people with him, as the skipper asked if there were any problemes. Tanja had seen them coming and had just told them what was going on and that one of the guests had said very quietly that two people cannot do it alone; they needed 3-4 helpers that are there now, Skip. Marion said: "Well if I cannot have these 4 people, I will get 4-6 other helpers." The cook said: "I am assistant cook Periér Jackés Periése and what gives you the rights to take away my helpers from me, as it pleases you? Who do you think you are, to do this?" The whole hall held its breath. Everyone heard how rude the cook was to head stewardess Marion! And he had said "you" to her in a rude tone.

I will complain, he said. The skipper asked who he wanted to complain to? Periése said to the head stewardess and I shouted: BINGO!! Then he said alright to the head steward. I shouted: BULLSEYE!! Well then, to the skipper, he said. From me came triple Bingo, triple Bullseye & Super Jackpot!!! Everyone in the hall was laughing now and the skipper asked: "Who is this woman?" Tanja quietly said, the same woman who saved us because of the kiosk sale. After the people in the hall finally calmed down Markus said to the temporary assistant cook, "You just insulted our head stewardess Marion in the presence of the skipper and the head steward by simply saying "You" to her in a rude tone and you were very unfriendly."

I ask myself, if this cook had anything to do with the accident of one of our ships cooks? He is unsympathetic and he scares me. I don't like him. Does he maybe have something to do with our luggage too? So that nobody can take a photo of him, or that I cannot follow him in my power wheelchair?

Chapter 2

The temporary assistant cook was gone again but without the four young people, they were helping Tanja with the kiosk sales. Marion said they almost lost me earlier. My power wheel-chair had been taken away from me. "Some-thing like that does not work at all Marion, do you know where it is right now," asked the skipper? "No," said Marion. The skipper asked me to come forward and said, isn't that the contest winner who is disabled? And who needs help with some things? Marion said I think so, I wasn't aware of that before. I will take care of her myself. Steffen, she said to the head steward, her hand luggage and that from all the other guests were taken away, the diabetics need their medication and she needs hers too. Steffen said I'll get it and make sure everyone gets their stuff. After I came forwards, I said that I had to go to the toilet again, Tanja went with me thistime, but I didn't tell her what I told Marion. In the mean time, the skipper discussed a few things with the crew before we returned. Tanja and I came back stood Markus with a wheelchair there for me from the ship's infirmary. No one had even noticed that Markus was gone at all. It also turned out that the cook didn't want anyone to have a cell phone so there would be no pictures of him, since the cook was a scammer wanted by Interpol. He was taken away with an escort and arrested until the police arrived.

Meanwhile the skipper helped with the distribution of the kiosk articles, he also decided that everything is free and the people who had already paid for the articles, got their money back. Then came the problem that it can get very cramped in the kitchen now because of the meal planning. There was a kind of game between the skipper and me, so many food suggestions came together. The kitchen was behind schedule with three cooks absent, so the cruise contest winners asked why not make cold platters of raw salads and do not forget the diabetic snacks. That was gladly accepted. The skipper and the head cook were so enthusiastic about my suggestions that they made me a guest cook. After a few minutes however, they took me out of the kitchen and asked me to help plan the menu for all the guests, along with Marion and her little sister Inga, who is the head of the diet kitchen, along with their niece Mary, who is the head of the vegetarian and vegan kitchen. But luckily, we only have a few vegans on board. Unfortunately I had to go to the toilet again because of my worries about my power wheelchair. It was so bad this time that I almost couldn't undress fast enough, only with help from Marion did it work in the last moment. Then Marion helped me stand up to get dressed and suddenly it went "puff" between the both of us, but I said: "Not here and not now," although it was very hard for me to say "No". Marion held me in her arms and kissed me, I allowed it. But we were still in the women's dress changing area of the kitchen. Marion's sister Inga just came into the room at that moment and I could have died cause of embarrassment, she just said congratulations both of you, but this is not the right place for that and then she took me in her arms for a moment and hugged me quickly. Because Marion had said, she would look after me and help me with the things I need help with, she also said she would bring me up in her cab-in. It was big and she said it is easier than going back and forth all the time. Both the head doc-tor and the head cook advised me to get some rest after going to the toilet 3 times in the last 1½ hours.

I finally got my power wheelchair back. The doctor said I should come by later, he would give me something against the bladder problems. Nothing came of that though, because we had to abandon the ship. Firstly, because there were problems with the power supply and a small fire so that Marion and I used the other wheelchair for our suitcases when we left the ship. Then there were these poisonous animals in the fruit deliveries, so that the zoo keepers and health officials could search for more of these animals. Then somewhere on the ship another fire broke out, the MS Lucky Charm was no longer operational. I wonder if this falsch cook had anything to do with these things too? I would say "Yes" if anyone asked me!

Chapter 3

We were accommodated in a hotel and holiday resort owned by the shipping company for a few days. The moment Marion said she would take care of me, the skipper made Tanja to head stewardess on probation, he and Marion had wanted to do that as a test for a long time, Marion said she was almost ready for the promotion. If Tanja handles these difficult problems well now, it's better than any made up test be-cause Marion isn't always there for her because of me. Tanja brought us under in the biggest bungalow there was. Marion and I were brought into one of the bedrooms with a bathroom. For Inga, Mary and herself were the other rooms and there was a guest room. Then I finally got something against my bladder problems.

Chapter 4

Here are the meal suggestions for the trip, yes there were now more of them: from hearty homemade cooking to good plain fare. From Apple strudel and Kaiserschmarrn, from Asia & India to the Far East! Just around the world!

Colorful basmati rice with diced peppers, radishes and herbs, plus pure schnitzel and for the vegetarians' tofu or vegetable burger. Other food suggestions are: Rheinish sauerbraten with raisins, knuckle of pork with sauerkraut, pizza, sweet corn, pork & baked beans, egg omelette, egg and potato pancakes, scrambled or fried eggs with spinach and potatoes, paella with seafood or chicken pieces, chicken fricassee, soy products, fries with sausages, salami, cured ham and cooked ham and many types of cheese, fish, stews. All sorts of noodles and pasta, stuffed vegetables. Noodles with meatballs, meatloaf. Maultaschen are filled noodle pockets. Minced meat and leek cream soup. Eggs with mustard sauce to pre- order. Stuffed mush-

rooms also to pre-order and all kinds of cabbage. Green cabbage with Sausages, spring
rolls, red apple cabbage, dumplings and sauerkraut with ribs. Greek salad. Fruit salads, raw
vegetable and other salads. Apple strudel with
powdered sugar and ice cream, savory waffles,
waffles with hot fruit and whipped cream, or
Kaiserschmarrn. Kalte hund= cold dog is one
package 250 g butter cookies and melted chocolate stapled in a baking pan first cookies then
chocolate with cookies back and forth about 7-8
times, ending with chocolate, then let it get cold.
All kinds of sheet cakes, pudding and yoghurt,
quark dishes, rice and much more.

  Yes like I said, the journey goes around the
world, also in the direction of Asia & India, the

Orient and the Far East. My food suggestions were all well received and were implemented very quickly. The replacement ship arrived after a few days, the MS Lucky Charm's sister ship, namely the Lucky Charm II. It is slightly larger than the first ship. After a few days we were able to continue our journey without any problems and with a larger crew, the skipper of the MS Lucky Charm II and his crew were responsible for the ship, the skipper and his crew of the Lucky Charm I were responsible for the program of events. All other crew members from both ships work hand in hand with each other throughout the ship. I had tried to bring my girlfriend and family onto the ship so that she could take care of me. Unfortunately, that didn't work out, so Marion continued to take care of me. That went quite well. One member who stayed was a social nurse because of me. But head stewardess Marion told the social nurse, when she asked if she should take care of me now no thanks, we've both gotten closer in the last few days and that I trust her. I was afraid she would say 'yes'. The nurse said fine, but if you have any questions you can come to me, I'm part of the crew, the head doctor had asked me to stay on board because of the diabetics and the disabled woman. Thank you for staying, said Marion. Well what can I say is, Marion and I have not become a couple for life, but for this journey and I have learned and experienced a lot that otherwise would not have been possible. It was a great time. At some point, every trip comes to an end, including these 4 weeks with arrival and departure. But since so much has happened, the shipping company has extended. Because almost everyone had booked a trip to the north, since for many people this trip should also be part of a world trip, the return trip to Hamburg would be a surprise for us; a new trip was attached and promised to catch up on the trip to the north later. They had also enabled me to stay on board for the return trip to Hamburg.

They had made it possible for everyone to see a few things in Hamburg, like the Miniature Wonderland or the Lion King, for some of us even both. They even paid for my return trip to Fulda and the special wheelchair taxi home from there. Marion and I are still friends and keep in touch. Tanja is now the second head stewardess alongside Marion and the two are now a happy couple. All the best wishes to both of you. Greet ings, Bunny.

APPENDIX:

Marion and Tanja have been back together for a while now and they are planning to get married. Both of them wanted me to be a bride woman and a witness for Marion. I'm so honored that they want me that I had to say: "YES!" They wanted to pay my fair so that I can come to them with my power wheelchair, they wanted to rent a special bus too, where I can drive into &

they are renting it for the whole time I am with them.

They had been together before I came on board the MS Lucky Charm I, after winning the four week Cruise contest. Both of them had a low point in their private life as a couple at this time and they threatened to separate forever. So they said: "We need a time out from our private lives, "but we still work together on the ship". They had no problem separating private life and work. Then I turned up as contest winner and this assistant cook showed up too.

In the short time that Marion cared for me on the ship, she and Tanja had time to find back to themselves. Marion had temporarily given up her job as head stewardess so that she could help and care for me. In this time, she and the skipper put Tanja up as head stewardess on probation, testing her if she could handle all of this and seeing how good she does the job. All the time until now, Tanja only knew the job out of second hand, behind and next to Marion. Now she had to handle all of this on her own. Of course, there was the head steward who she can ask to help if needed, he changed his duty plan so that he and Tanja work together. Not on ly did Marion and the Skipper think that Tanja was almost ready for a promotion, head steward Steffen thought that too! This test will show if they are right. I don't know if Tanja ever found out that Marion had asked the head steward to please do that. The skipper had also said, yes please do that and keep an eye on Tanja, help her if needed. In addition, Marion was still there too but not so often, because she was caring for me. She brought me under in her cabin because it was big and she had a bathtub and a shower so that she could help me all the time and not have to go over half of the ship to help me. Later she did the same on the Lucky Charm II. Brought us together in the same cabin for the same reason, so that she could help me at any time.

Tanja was doing so well in her job as second head stewardess that the skipper made her to that officially before we got onto the Lucky Charm II, but he did not tell anyone on that day.

He told everyone about it a few weeks after we all got back home.

A very large reward was offered for the capture of the cook sought by INTERPOL and the crew of the M S Lucky Charm I got it for exposing the scammer. Thanks to the crew, they could finally arrest him. That is the only reason why Marion and Tanja could not only invite me and rent the special bus, but also pay for my boat ticket. They also put me up in their big cabin of course, so they could both take care of me; they were both so grateful because they said that I had brought them back together again. Tanja had also found out that Marion's job as head stewardess is a very hard job and Marion found out that it is not so easy to help someone then she had once thought, you just can't say ok I will help you, there also has to be trust between the person who needs help with personal things like bathing and the person who is helping or trying to help. Especially if one of these persons is handicapped. However, the time together with me helped both of them they said. And this surprise was there way to say Thank You to me! It was a wonderful time with both them, I am so happy for both of them. Forever your friend, Bunny.

THE END

Novel #2: Brief description:

It's about Respect, love and the relationship be
tween two women and the resulting affection
even with sexuality in the background, loyalty &
fidelity, courage & humility, friendship, trust,
obedience, modesty & bravery and the willingness to help! But most of all dealing with everyday life with all of it's good and bad times over
all ages, from childhood until adult age, especially with some things sounding like they cannot be true, because they are so fantastic like
out of a bad movie and still some of it could be
true or not! The Story itself is Fantasy, but judge
on your own what is fantasy & what could be
true.

1956

Novel #2:

My encounter with the High Priestess Helena – or love at first sight.

Chapter 1

My encounter with the High Priestess was brief but memorable. I was at an event when chaos broke out. She was there to. The young woman next to me was very beautiful and was quickly taken away. As she walked past me, our eyes met and it was love at first sight! She had been taken away so quickly that her handbag and jacket had been left behind. I grabbed them and put them in my backpack. I knew I had to find this woman no matter how or where. I wasn't thinking about sex with this woman at that moment, only that I love her. (A few hours later I found out her name is Helena.) I didn't even know who she was at that time, but I fell in love with her. I have no idea where to look for her either, but I need to find her! I had put her handbag in my backpack; (But did I think to search her handbag for an ID card? Of course not! There was no time to do this, I had to flee). She had left her things behind as the chaos broke out. I wanted to give her the things back. (I wonder if her look meant, please help me as our eyes met? I don't know.) I left the room right after the woman but she was gone. I could only try to get out safely. I ran and as I was trying to pull up a stair bridge to slow down the pursuers a little, two young men came up to me and said:

"Please come with us, we'll get you out safely."

A third young man took my backpack and said:

"I can't find the things, Michael; there gone as if

someone had taken them away." Michael was

not under the group of people that had taken

the young woman away. He would have thought

for sure that I might have the things they are

looking for if he had seen me in that room.

Again I wanted to ask what was going on but

there wasn't any time for questions, as we now

needed to get away from the Chaos Hall and the

venue. (Too bad, that would have saved a lot of

time and nerves.) I saw Michael say something

to a group of men and women standing to one

side and then he came back to us. The group

walked back to the venue and Michael said again no time for questions. Unfortunately.

I entered the vestibule of a large complex and was led to a fireplace near the entrance, where I was offered tea. Michael and his team were suddenly gone. Then after drinking tea, I was asked to please take my shoes off and if I can't walk in socks, these too. They took these and my backpack too, so that I couldn't tell them that I had something in it that wasn't mine. I was taken to the second fireplace, where they washed my feet and gave me sandals, that's when I realized I was in a temple. I had just been told that I had been invited into a temple, but that also means I cannot refuse a ceremony if I want to go to the next room in the temple. A cleansing ritual with very precise processes; First, it was the tea I was given and second they took me further from the fireplace into the room, near a large pool of water and stripped me down to my underwear. Because not only I have to be clean, but also my laundry. After standing there a short time in my underwear, with the three guards who had been guiding me now standing behind and beside me, I was blindfolded. I had a hunch of what to expect, but I wasn't entirely sure. I just wanted to wait and see what happens. Then someone stood in front of me again and very gently stripped off my panties and my top together with the open bra, as it closes in the front. Otherwise, I would have had to stretch my arms either back or up. But since I was wearing a shirt under the bra, they came off together. My eyes were blindfolded, I couldn't see anything, but I felt that whoever this person is; that 'she' or 'he' was very careful and it was so absolutely quiet in the whole room, you could hear a pin drop.

My laundry was taken away by someone and I didn't dare to move for fear of falling, but I felt a cool breeze on my skin. After what felt like an eternity to me, the blindfold was removed and I fell to my knees at the same moment, because standing in front of me in all her naked beauty was the woman I had fallen in love with! The woman I thought I had to save. As I fell, I breathed softly almost in a whisper, "Are you a priestess?" Someone said: "She's not just a priestess, she's our high priestess." Nobody would have thought that I was born under the sign of Aries; I was more devout than a lamb. "Are you the person who invited me to the temple?" I asked whispering. As she said yes I just thought, this is beyond my thinking. I bowed my head and lowered my eyes even more and said: "My lady and mistress, what do you command me?"

The priestess came and knelt in front of me, first she said please look up to me that was not easy to do, she did not touch my body but she took my hands in hers and said please get up, but I couldn't do it by myself, I had no strength and said so. She pulled me up with the help of the guards and looked at me for a few moments. "You have to come to me in the big pool to get anormal bath first and then get a ritual bath for purification of the soul, if you want to go to the next room with me tonight. Your laundry must be cleaned too. I sent my guards to find you. Michael saw you at the gate, that's how he was able to find you so quickly." I asked: "You looked for me, why?" The priestess said: "Because I really wanted to see you again", that was her answer. "I wanted to see you again too," I said. "I am afraid, but I will obey whatever you command me," I added shaking. She held my hands tighter saying: "You don't have to be afraid; I'm with you all the time. Come on get up again now please try, we will help you. Trust me." I had fallen to my knees again. She was still holding my hands, her grip was as hard as steel, mine was hard too. That's good and taking my hands even tighter in hers. She very slowly got up off the Floor; she was on her feet in front of me and was gently pulling me up to her. The three guards were also holding me tighter now too.

When she was sure that I was standing now, the priestess let go of me and took a few steps to the side. She looked at me again for a few minutes just letting me stand there naked in front of her with only our eyes meeting, being held by the three guards who try so hard not to touch my body to much. I looked at her too, forgetting everything else that was going on around me. She is so beautiful! Her body is flaw

less!

Backing away a little she was turning around
and saying please bring her to the pool, leading
the way. She was already in the pool waiting to
help me in when I got there. Then she began
helping me to prepare for the ritual. It was ex-
actly as I had imagined. First, my mistress had
bathed herself with soap then she bathed me
giving me a normal bath with soap, kissing me
gently and touching my body for the first time
knowing that I was afraid, trying to comfort me
down. Then it was our turn for the ritual bath to
cleanse our body & soul and I was very afraid of
that. She was also nervous just like me. But I
was not really ready for the next step. I've been

trying to control my panic because I'm scared of men when it comes to sexuality and I told this to my mistress. "To get into the next room with me, you have to endure this ritual," she said softly, holding me in her arms because I was shaking so much. This scares me terribly. The thought of what's to come makes me panic, even with my mistress next to me, because bathing and cleaning inside and out, means we have to bathe with the men, or rather they bathe us, this is what I was thinking at least and that scares me even more. The high priest has now entered the ante-chamber. The high priestess told her Lord and Master that I am very scared to bathe with men, because I am afraid to have sex with them, thinking it had something to do with the ritual (and I should be right!) He said hewould think about it and then the ritual began.

The three guards and our master, yes I also re garded him as my master, had begun to bathe my mistress and me. Two of the guards bathed my lady, the third guard and our high priest bathed me just like my mistress had done too, with soap. Bathing was clear to me, but ritual bathing to cleanse the soul means we had to drink a witch's brew that tasted so shitty it al- most made us throw up. The only reason that wedidn't throw up was because the men were holding us, but we had to drink it so that our bodies could be flushed out. It scared the hell out of me, but my Mistress was here on my side, with her endless patience she not only helped me overcome my fear and panic, she even helped me to do things that I never even dreamed of before. I was also scared about my mistress because I don't know if she knows that I fell in love with her. And I don't know if she had fallen in love with me either? Do we both feel the same for each other and can that go well?

Chapter 2

The first part of the ritual was over; the second part said that a motif of something should be tattooed into our skin to show that we belong together; because we found out that, we do love each other. I was asked what I think is beautiful and I said roses! Perhaps I can have a rose bud that is just opening and my mistress has a rose that has already opened because she is more experienced in these things than I am. At least I thought that she was. The First Letter of our names should also be in the roses, they said.

That's when they found out that my name is Berta and my nickname is Bunny, that's when I found out that my mistress's name is Helena. Hence the "B" and the "H". I was scared but I didn't want to say no, I didn't want to disappoint Helena.

 My mistress had lost a baby sometime before the event. She wanted to distract herself by going there. Now I could finally tell Helena that I had put her handbag and jacket in my backpack, "I've wanted to say that since we left the

venue but there hadn't been time to tell anyone." I said. Suddenly stood Helena there laugh
ing in a beautiful clear voice: "I should have
known that after our eyes met and I saw the
backpack in your hands, that you would pick up
my things and try everything to bring them back
to me. And you beautiful woman did just that!
But not only that, you did much more. You did
everything that was asked of you, not even
knowing that I was here until I stood naked before you. And just the same, you brought my
things back. Although I did not leave them there
on purpose. But by the time I thought you might
have my things in your backpack, it was too late
to ask and too late to stop the ritual. You were
already standing there stripped down to your

underwear and blindfolded. Now please tell me honestly, would you have gone through the ritual if you had told me before that you have my things?" I stood there fighting against my tears; I looked at her direct in her eyes and then bowed my head deeper than before. I lowered my eyes deeper too. "I love you my Lady, is that answer enough", I asked softly and gently? She took my head in her hands, turned my face up to her and kissed me hard but still gently on my lips and held me tight against her beautiful wet body. I didn't dare to move; I just stood there in front of her and was just as wet, standing up to our breasts in the pool. We just stood there she kissing me, and I letting it happen, but not knowing where to put my hands or my arms. Helena just put my arms around her neck, and held me even tighter then before, and I felt her hot tears on my face, so I just hugged her tighter too, so she knew that I'm there for her, because this time she was the one who was scared.

She still had the hormones in her body that stimulates the milk production, Heaven only knows why. I think this ritual revived everything, because suddenly after we finished the first part of the ritual, my mistress started convulsing and bleeding, I screamed around at everyone and immediately everybody started running all over the place. The medicine woman first brought her something to drink, a mixture out of painkillers and sedatives and something to stop the heavy bleeding. It could not stop the bleeding completely, but it might make it weaker. With much persuasion and patience on my behalf, she drank it down after I said the mix couldn't be worse than what we both had to drink at the ritual, I just took a sip of it myself. Suddenly it turned out that she still had a baby in her womb and not just the one she had lost earlier in the day. As a result, the doctors did everything they could to save the baby and I just prayed, which was very, very wild but I did not care about that.

Chapter 3

"The woman should just stay alive God please, I just found her today. I do not want to lose her this way, her family needs her and I need her too. It was love at first sight, I had hoped to get to know her, maybe even become friends and eat cake or ice cream with her. Alternatively got to the park or to the cinema. Sex was far, far away for me at that moment, not even on my mind. But only if she stays alive, can we do this. Lord God, Father in heaven, you have already taken a child from her today, your kingdom come, your will be done, on earth as it is in heaven. Forgive me, my sin for falling in love with this beautiful woman, as I am terrified of men. Please put this woman out of her torment and let her and the child live; and get or stay healthy. For yours is the kingdom, the power, the glory of heaven and the honor for justice forever, Amen.

Only you Lord, knows whether mother and child live or die. I wish that they both live, but who am I to try to talk like that? Just a six-year-old girl. A child who was so sick that they put her in the dying room of the hospital, a girl that could see the light at the end of the tunnel, she's almost there, can feel the warmth, and then she gets pulled back into the cold. Into the dark cold world of the here and now. Brought back only through God's grace and mercy. For a mother's infinite love which was stronger than death. This six-year-old girl was born again, but not as the healthy girl she once was, but as a child, completely paralyzed from neck to toe and blind.

She was blind for just 7 weeks but paralyzed for the rest of her life. This child from back then, who spent decades wondering why me? She never stopped fighting no matter what; not even after her father had told her that if she didn't start using her right hand, just like the left hand, he would get the ax and chop it off because she didn't need it if she wasn't using it.

It had taken a long time until the day she finally realized that this is what the fight was all about. No matter how sick you are, no matter how bad things are for you, someone is always worse off then you! This humble child of yore, who can only kneel here today by your merciful grace, flees for the life of this woman and her child, Oh Lord."

Chapter 4

"Woman who was reborn as a child, are you ready to take care of this woman and her child?" A powerful voice suddenly thundered through the antechamber! There was also a bright flash of light! Trembling very badly for fear I said modestly, „Yes, oh Lord I am." Then suddenly an angel stood there speaking in name of our Lord Father in heaven. "Child who was born again, you are so naked as the Lord created you, so is the woman you ask for, whom you are standing next to, but why is this third woman and the eight men who are with you naked too?" the Angel asked. "Great Lord, we had just finished a ritual bath for the purification of the soul when my mistress collapsed. I had to do this ritual in order to be allowed to go further into the temple where my mistress wants me to go with her. The third woman and six of the men are part of the purification ritual the other two men joined us as my mistress came into labor.

Dear God, if I had a few humble wishes to ask, one of them would be that this woman and her baby live and that the woman recovers and stays as healthy as before and that no one is blinded by the sight of your angel or by your sight Lord please."

Chapter 5

"Quick blankets that we can put around my mistress to get her warm and we need some leather and reins, so we can make a kind of makeshift harness with straps, to put the child on the mother's body and strap it down, then cover both of them to keep them warm.

God, please let everything go well"! Now elder born woman, you are brave and humble, do you still have any more wishes? "If you could fulfill my desires that I have already said please Lord that is more than enough for me. Please oh Lord, let the people in this room who know what to do, take care of the baby and let me take care of the mother. She is so cold that I want to keep her warm with my body." I said. "Woman who was born again your wishes will be granted, but why did you lower your eyes and now you have been blindfolded?" asked the angel. "Great Lord, it is not my right to look into your holy face. There was a time when your angel come to the Virgin Mary to announce that she would conceive your Son Jesus Christ, or when you told Noah to build the Arch, or when you told Moses to climb the Mountain to receive the 10 Commandments, or when the angel came to the shepherds in the fields, to announce the birth of Jesus Christ and other Bible events. Back then, people had a very different attitude toward you, they believed in you my Lord. But today people are afraid of you. Once I was blind as a child; I don't want to be blind again because I saw your holy face."

"Does this child already have a name?" the angel asked. "I don't think so lord; the woman didn't even know that she had another child in her womb, since you took her other child earlier to-day", Medicine woman Lucy said this sadly. So no one has a name for the girl. "I have a name", I said softly. I was asked what this name is? "Angel", I said. Yes, that's a very good name, everybody agreed.

Suddenly my mistress and I cried out, both of us looking at the roses we had talked about a while back that day. Branded into our skin, for me the opening rosebud with an "H" in it for Helena and for her the rose in full blossom with a "B" in it for either Berta or Bunny. Which ever Helena wanted to call me. But the roses were not made in the same way the temple people wanted to do them namely pricked, but instead they are branded by the Lord in Heaven himself.

Medicine woman do you have mountain ash? Yes, my Lord. Then treat the arms of the two women with it. The child should also get the letters "B" & "H" on her arms. "Please don't Heavenly Father, the child is still very weak, with the letters 'B' & 'H' she will definitely be teased, you have 'breast holders' on your arms and HB was a German cigarettes brand, "Don't go up into the air, get yourself a HB and calm down." That's how the TV & Radio advertisement went. I wouldn't even put the roses on the child's skin, please God." Well then not the letters, but the roses yes. As a birthmark, the bud is placed in the center of the rose that is full in blossom. "My Lord, thy Will be done! "I said maybe the child's name could be changed to Angel-Linn then nobody can tease her about her name. Like'angel' (engel) with a B in front (Bengel), equal to Brat. She doesn't deserve that".

Chapter 6

Finally we got into the next room, Helena and I could lie down on an artificial lawn. We can finally rest as we have already received the roses from God, showing that we are together now. Lucy has pumped Helena's milk for the baby; she cannot give the child her breast very long at the moment, so the milk is pumped up and held in reserve. Helena and I are lying together on a air mattress trying to warm up. We're together now, but neither of us knows what's to come.

Now it's just a matter of getting our strength back and thanking God, we're alive. We can only hope and pray that Angel-Linn finds the strength to survive. Thank you Lord God for every day you give us to live. Amen.

Chapter 7

Helena and I have now warmed up and we are starting to get to know each other. Angel-Linn is doing a little better, in incubation and connected to many electronics. Lucy brought in additional professionals who know about childcare. An ad joining room in the temple has been converted into an infirmary especially for Angel-Linn and the child care people are located in a room next door. Helena and I stay close by and can finally get dressed again, laugh. But not in street clothes while we are in the temple, only in the white robes of the temple and underwear. I got a new bra; the bra I wore before the ritual is black so I got a new white bra. I wanted to pay for the bra but Lucy said: "no you don't have to that's ok, it's a gift from Helena for you."

I was asked what kind of animals I like, I said cats and horses. Then Helena told me that among other horses, she also has Thoroughbreds in her stables and now I know why Helena has such a steel hard grip. It's because of the Thoroughbreds! I don't know yet if they are English- or Arabian Thoroughbreds, the one is even harder to handle then the other. But I think with her steel grip, that she has Arabian Thoroughbreds. I told Helena that I also rode once. Thera-py riding on prescription, for a short time. Hele-na said she would take me to the stables later if I wanted, when she and I got better. Later I found out that she has won many prizes, ribbons and trophies with the Thoroughbreds and with the other horses too.

We were just talking about my childhood and Helena asked me if the things about the dying room and the light at the end of the tunnel when I was about six where true? She asked if this thing with the ax was also really true too. I said yes to everything. This thing with the ax; was when I was about seven years old, same as when I was between 17 and 18, as my father told me I was a slut, a whore, a bitch and that I was also a lesbian, because I wasn't interested in boys. By God not until I was between 16 and 17 did anyone really know that I was a girl with my short hair cut; until this time I did not even have breasts! I was as flat as a board! On the other hand, my father said: "Woe to you, if you come home with a child in your womb, I'll kill you both!" He was serious; he meant it just like that; just like he did with the ax! As I had just turned 15, I had a great loss, three weeks after my 15th birthday my mother Lucy died. When I was 17 years old, I lived with my father step-mother and my little brother Kurt. According to my nationality and where I lived in the United States namely California, I wasn't of legal age until I turned age 21. About three years later, my father blamed me for my mother's death, "If you had died then at the ageof six, your mother would still be alive today! He also blamed me for trying to poison my family when I was a child."

I broke down after telling this story. Then Helena took me in her arms and held me for a while. Afterwards, Helena told me that she was very young when her mother & father died in a car accident, that she had survived and that the high priest is her Uncle, godfather and guardian.

We held each other in our arms and cried our eyes out until we had no more tears. After a while we both felt better, lying arm in arm in bed next to each other in our room until we fell asleep. When we woke up, we were so sweaty that we had to take a shower to get our heads cool and our bodies clean. To calm down like Helena said. Later Helena said, let's go to the stable, I laughed yes we will have to bathe in hot water or get a hot shower afterwards again lol, but it doesn't matter. Let's go past the kitchen and get some carrots, apples and dry bread or rolls for the horses. In addition, a bunch of radishes. For the horses too, asked Helena surprised? No laugh for me, I said. I'm hungry.

Bunny, I think I have to ask you what you like to eat, lol. Helena I think it would be easier to ask what I don't like. That would be:

Mushrooms, Brussels sprouts, salsify, kohlrabi, mustard, meatballs with capers, sea radish, onions, eggs in mustard sauce, buttermilk, kefir, cottage cheese, camembert, herring and rollmopse are types of fish that I don't like.

I love: tuna, pasta with minced meat, pasta with meatballs, rice, meatloaf, all other kinds of pasta too, pizza, feta cheese sheep yes – feta cheese goat no laugh, potato pancakes, mashed potatoes, peas, carrots, radish, sweet corn, scrambled or fried eggs with spinach and potatoes, pork with baked beans, kidney beans, bell peppers, tomatoes, black and green olives, Emmental cheese, Gouda and cheddar cheese, salami, ham and eggs, bacon & eggs, minced meat leeks and celery, gyros, sauerbraten from beef, etc.

Yes Bunny, you are right said Helena and started laughing crystal clear.

Chapter 8

We are in the stables now. I wasn't ready for it at all even though she said it after the shower. I said let's go to the kitchen on the way out, because it wasn't that long back that Angel-Linn was born, but the doctors said if she takes it easy she'll be fine. She had beautiful horses in the stable; she didn't only have the Thoroughbreds. Helena wanted the horses to get used to my voice and smell. And I should get used to the horses too. Helena wanted the horses to get to know me. That is why she brought me together with one of her smaller horses. When I touched it, I noticed she had a thick hot leg and said that. The vet was in the stables as one of the other smaller haflinger mares had just foaled and was called over. Helena and the vet let me hold the skiddy mare; both of them standing next to me; Helena was sure I could handle this, the vet was not so sure but he trusted Helena. The horse was scared and in pain but I spoke to her in a calm voice petting her very gently and calming her down. The vet noticed that she had a horseshoenail in her hoof. The vet gave the horse an injection and rinsed the wound and then he cut out the horseshoe nail, cleaned the wound and bandaged the hoof and leg after put-ting medicine on the hoof and leg to draw out the infection and to keep the hoof clean and dry.

Helena and I smelled so much like horses and
medicine ourselves that we both had to take a
shower in the bath tub again, because this time
standing under the shower was not enough,
laugh.

Chapter 9

Christmas is coming soon. Helena & I are going to get engaged and Angel-Linn is going to
get baptized. The high priest already told us that
he wants to baptize the child with the Name:
"Angel-Linn Edith Rose Chrissy." If this name
was okay for both of us. The two of them had already made me the godmother and guardian of
the child as a Christmas surprise. Early on
Christmas Eve, Helena took me to the stables

blindfolded again, but this time she was guiding me together with the vet who was also a Family member as I learned with the time. Helena said she has two surprises that might interest me. After we reached the stables she led me first to the haflinger mare that had foaled on the day we had met. The young filly was doing great and Helena said that the little one will be Angel-Linn's horse as they were born on the same day. Helena then said that the name of the filly is: "Bunny's Angel!" I could not believe what I had just heard.

Then they blindfolded me again and led me to a big new box, with Helena saying stay right here. She said something to someone then she turned to me, took off the blindfold and gave me an apple, saying Merry Christmas my love here is your gift from me, well at least one of them. Blue Angel Star is now your horse dear, together with the foal she is carrying. You saved her life a few months ago and I saw how you love her, you only had eyes for her until Steve gave her the shot, after that you where there for us again. Here is another apple. I didn't know what to say and Helena saw that I wanted to fall on my knees again and she grabbed me saying: "No!" So I just bowed my head looking down on the floor. She took my head once again gently in her hands pulling my face up and kissing me. Then she said come we have to bathe and get ready for the ceremony with Angel-Linn as you are her godmother. And Uncle Joey will announce our engagement too.

THE END

About the Author:

B. E. Wasner was born on March 30, 1953 in Frankfurt Main, Germany; as the daughter of an US Army soldier and a nurse. She was named <u>Berta </u>Edith Schulz. About 6 months later, she and her parents moved back to the USA. B. E. lived from 1953-1956 in Conneticut, USA. In 1956 the family moved to Panama. There in 1958 she got sick with brain-fever and almost died. After recovering awhile in 1959, the family moved to San Francisco, California, USA. In 1960 they moved up near Santa Rosa, California where they lived till New Year's Eve 1962. From there they moved to Giessen, Germany till April 1966. Then back home again near Santa

Rosa, until they finally came back to Germany in October 1969.

First again in Frankfurt Main, then in 1971 farther north. In 1975 B.E. came to city where she still lives today. On June 30. 1976 B. E. got married to Mr. Wasner and in 1981 they where divorced. Since Aug. 2002 she lives with her male cat that was born in May 2002. He is a Maine Coon & Siamese mix. In the 1980s she got the German citizenship. She has been disabled since she was six years old and has been stuck in a wheelchair for about 1½ years. B.E. speaks English & German.

In 200...plus B.E. wrote a short story as part of an online RPG. In 201..plus she stopped playing the RPG with her Friends. 2016 she wrote the next part of the RPG 'Just for Fun'! Then when she was seriously thinking about writing a book in 2021-2022 she wrote part 3 of her RPG. A science fiction fantasy dream. 2021 she also had a second fantasy dream that she brought to paper. And 2022 she brought 3 role plays and Résumé-The Story of my Life to paper and to print in German. Now the Stories are coming out in English too. Starting in October 2022, with "Can Dreams Come True.-Or Love At First Sight!"